Mabel Ran Away with the Toys

Jan Wahl
illustrated by Liza Woodruff

🐾 Whispering Coyote
A Charlesbridge Imprint

To Lee Murray with love
—J.W.

For Maggie, Max, and Paul with many thanks
—L.W.

A **Whispering Coyote** Book
Published by Charlesbridge Publishing
85 Main Street
Watertown, MA 02472
(617) 926-0329
www.charlesbridge.com

Library of Congress Cataloging-in-Publication Data

Wahl, Jan.
    Mabel ran away with the toys / Jan Wahl ; illustrated by Liza Woodruff.
       p. cm.
    Summary: A young girl is happy with her parents and her toys, but things
change when her baby brother is born.
       ISBN 1-58089-059-8 (reinforced for library use)
       ISBN 1-58089-067-9 (softcover)
    [1. Babies—Fiction. 2. Brothers and sisters—Fiction. 3. Toys—Fiction.]
I. Woodruff, Liza, ill. II. Title.

PZ7.W1266Mab2000
[E]—dc21
                                                    00-024591

Printed in Hong Kong
(hc) 10 9 8 7 6 5 4 3 2 1
(sc) 10 9 8 7 6 5 4 3 2 1

Illustrations done in pen and ink and watercolors on 140 lb. Arches cold
press watercolor paper
Display type and text type set in Goudy Old Style Bold
Separated and manufactured by Regent Publishing Services
Book production by *The Kids at Our House*
Designed by *The Kids at Our House*

MABEL lived a good life.

She lived with her mother and father, and Mrs. Lion, Remsen Rat, and One-Eyed Wolf.

At breakfast, Mabel and her parents ate and talked. Mrs. Lion, Remsen Rat, and One-Eyed Wolf sat quietly, watching.

In her room, however, the toys sometimes had things to say.

"My back needs scratching," said Mrs. Lion.

"Something is in my eye,"
said One-Eyed Wolf.
"My tail is tied in a knot,"
added Remsen Rat.

Often on Sundays, everybody rode around in the red car.

Once, they lay in the sand at beautiful
Treasure Island.

At vacation time, Mabel, her parents,
and her toys rode on donkeys through the
Grand Canyon. Mrs. Lion got hiccups.

In the spring, they went to the zoo. Mabel took Mrs. Lion. Her mother took One-Eyed Wolf. Mabel's father took Remsen Rat.

The animals made noises. The toys sat silent. Mabel and her parents shared cotton candy. It was a good life.

Then one day Mabel's mother went off to
the hospital. When her mother came back, she
brought a new baby named Noah.

Now, in the middle of the night, there was the sound of a baby loudly crying.

"It wakes me up,"
said Mrs. Lion.
The wolf and rat agreed.

Often, Mabel heard her mother sing softly to Noah. Mabel got up to tell her father, "We can't sleep."

"You cried too when you were a baby," said her father. "Phooey," Remsen Rat whispered in her ear.

Next morning, Mabel sighed. "The toys and I are moving to the playhouse. It's not noisy there," she said.

"I'm sorry to see you go," said Mabel's mother, smiling.

"Would you like to say goodbye to Noah?"
asked her father. So she did.

Noah was quiet. But again he started to yell
loudly. One-Eyed Wolf blinked.

Mabel stretched out with the toys on the rug. "This is peaceful," she said.

"So peaceful," the toys agreed. Mabel tried to take a nap.

Suddenly, *thump, baroom!*

It began to pour. "It was nicer at home,"
said Mabel. The toys listened as raindrops beat
on the roof.

Wind shook the playhouse. Lightning
flashed. Thunder roared. Mabel huddled close
to the toys.

"I hope Noah has a warm
blanket," Mabel said.
The rain was pounding.
Mabel saw her father
at the kitchen window.
"I wonder what Noah is doing.
He doesn't know about rain!
He might be scared," Mabel said.
She told the toys: "I'm moving back.
Are you coming?" But the lion, the
wolf, and the rat didn't want to get wet.

Mabel dashed to the house.
Quickly, her father opened the
kitchen door.

"I need a glass of juice," said Mabel, coming in. "A good idea," replied her father. Then he dried her wet hair.

Mabel tiptoed upstairs where Noah lay
in his crib. She sat on her mother's lap,
waiting for Noah to cry. Then Mabel could
sing him to sleep.

The rain stopped. Mabel's father brought
the toys in. They wanted to see Noah.
    "Will he want cheese?" asked Remsen Rat.
    "He needs more hair," said Mrs. Lion.
    "He's okay—for a baby," grunted
One-Eyed Wolf.

And they listened to Mabel's song.